A JOURNEY THROUGH TIME

NEFERTARI
PRINCESS OF EGYPT

Published in the United States of America by

Oxford University Press, Inc.

198 Madison Avenue

New York, NY 10016

Oxford is a registered trademark of Oxford University Press, Inc.

ISBN 0-19-521507-9

© 1998 Istituto Geografico De Agostini S.p.A., Novara

English text © 1998 British Museum Press

Published in Great Britain in 1998 by British Museum Press

Published in Italy as *A Spasso Con ... Nefertari, Principessa d'Egitto*

Printed in Italy by Officine Grafiche, Novara, 1998

Text and illustrations: Roberta Angeletti

A JOURNEY THROUGH TIME...

NEFERTARI
PRINCESS OF EGYPT

by Roberta Angeletti

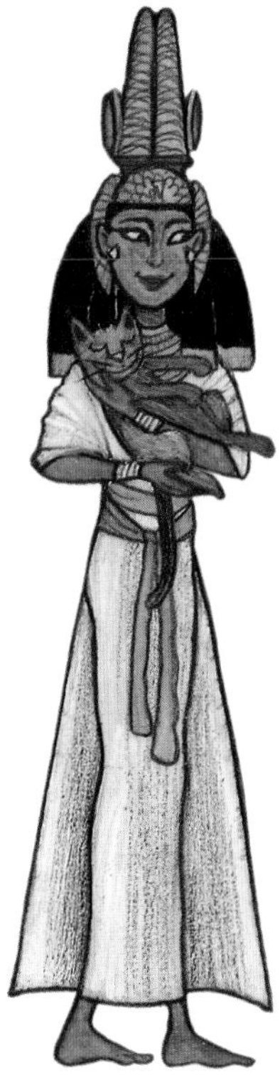

Oxford University Press
New York

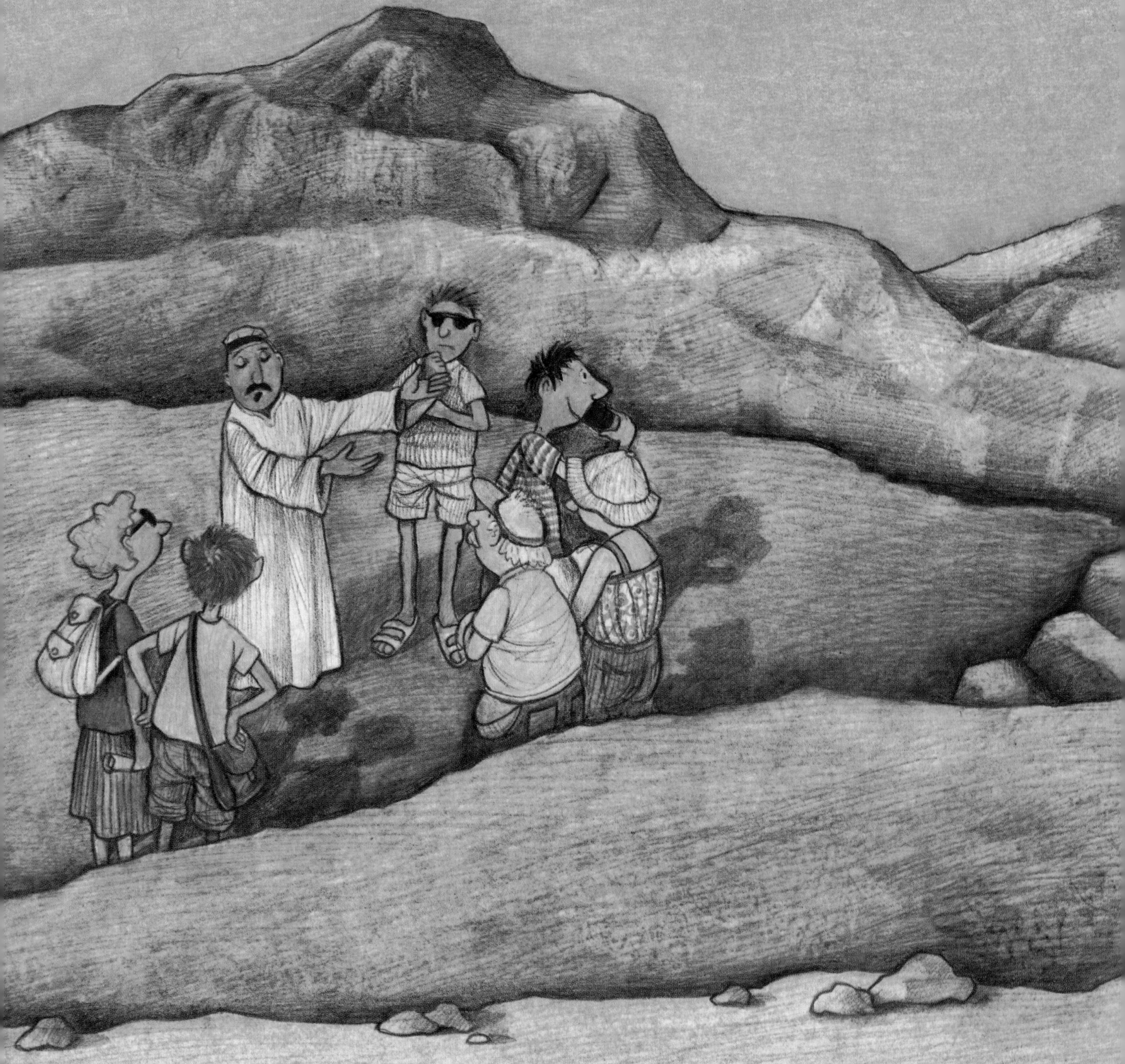

Hello! My name's Anna, and at school I'm famous for my amazing stories! My teacher says I make them up, but I promise that what I'm going to tell you is true... It all started when I went on holiday to Egypt with my Mom and Dad. One day our group visited a place called the Valley of the Queens.

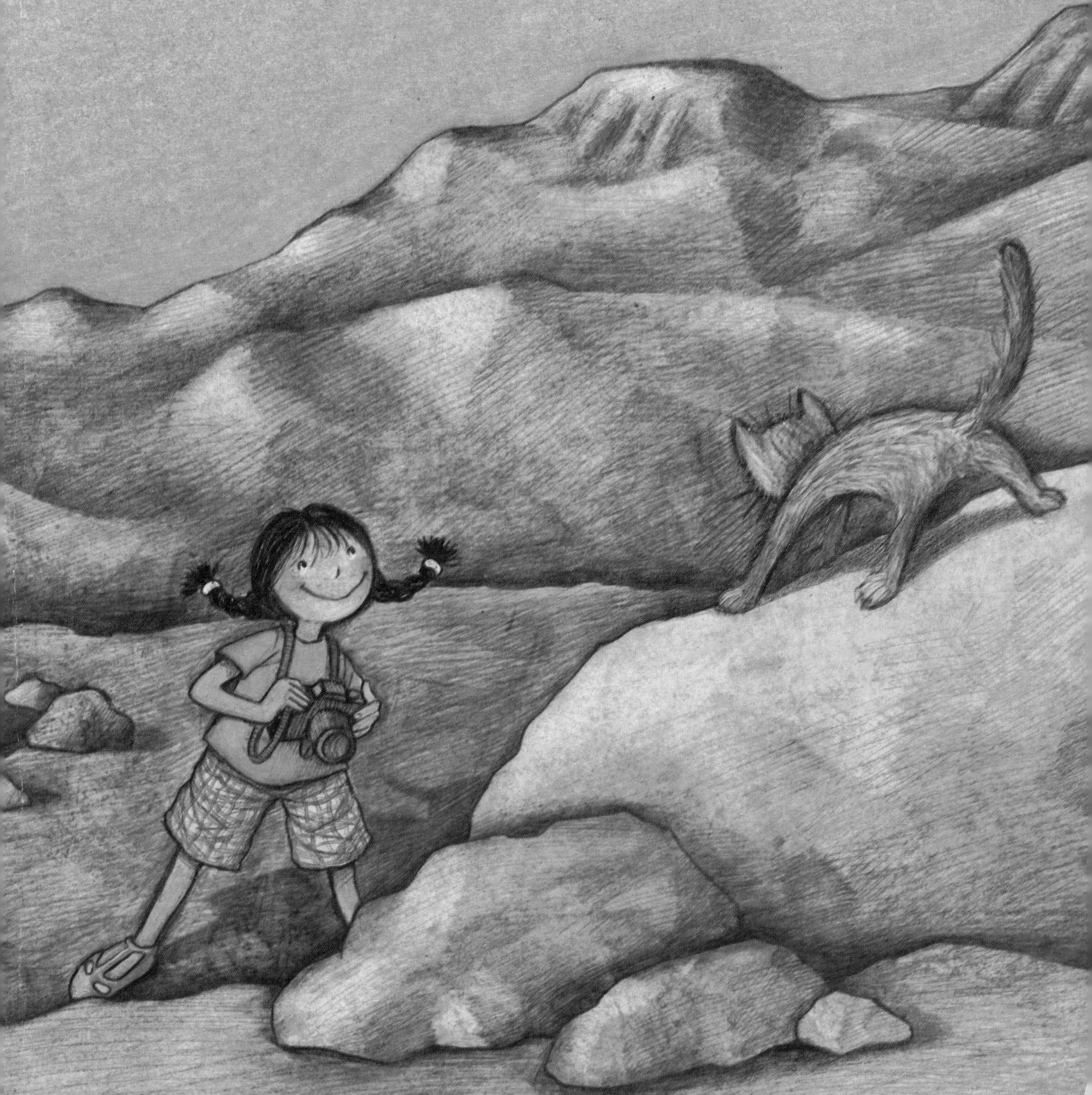

Our guide was working very hard. “Here, ladies and gentlemen you can see ... To your left you can admire ...” I’m sure that what he was saying was very interesting, but with the hot Egyptian sun beating down on our heads, it wasn’t easy to concentrate. While we were standing there I saw a pretty gray pussycat playing in the sun.

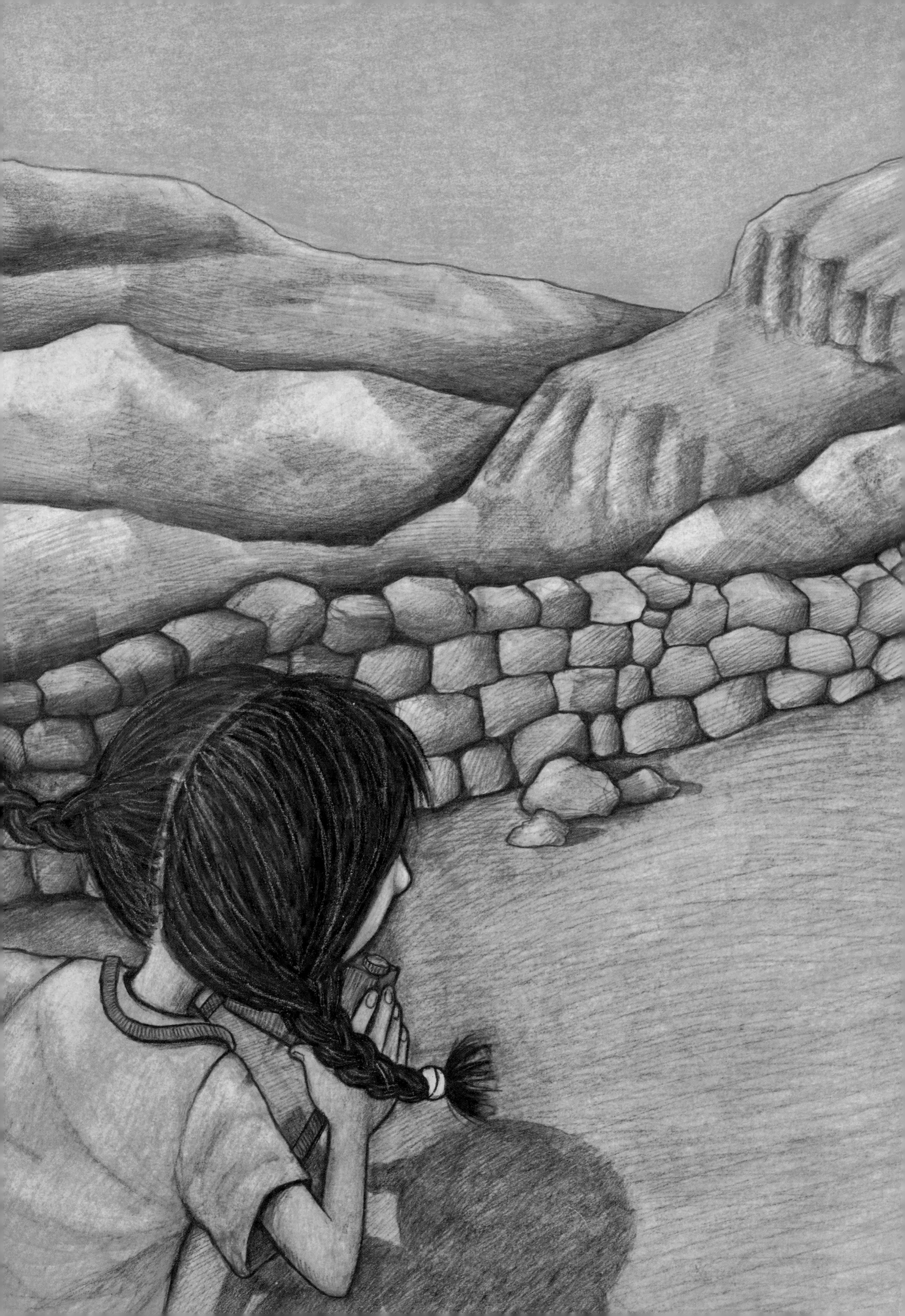

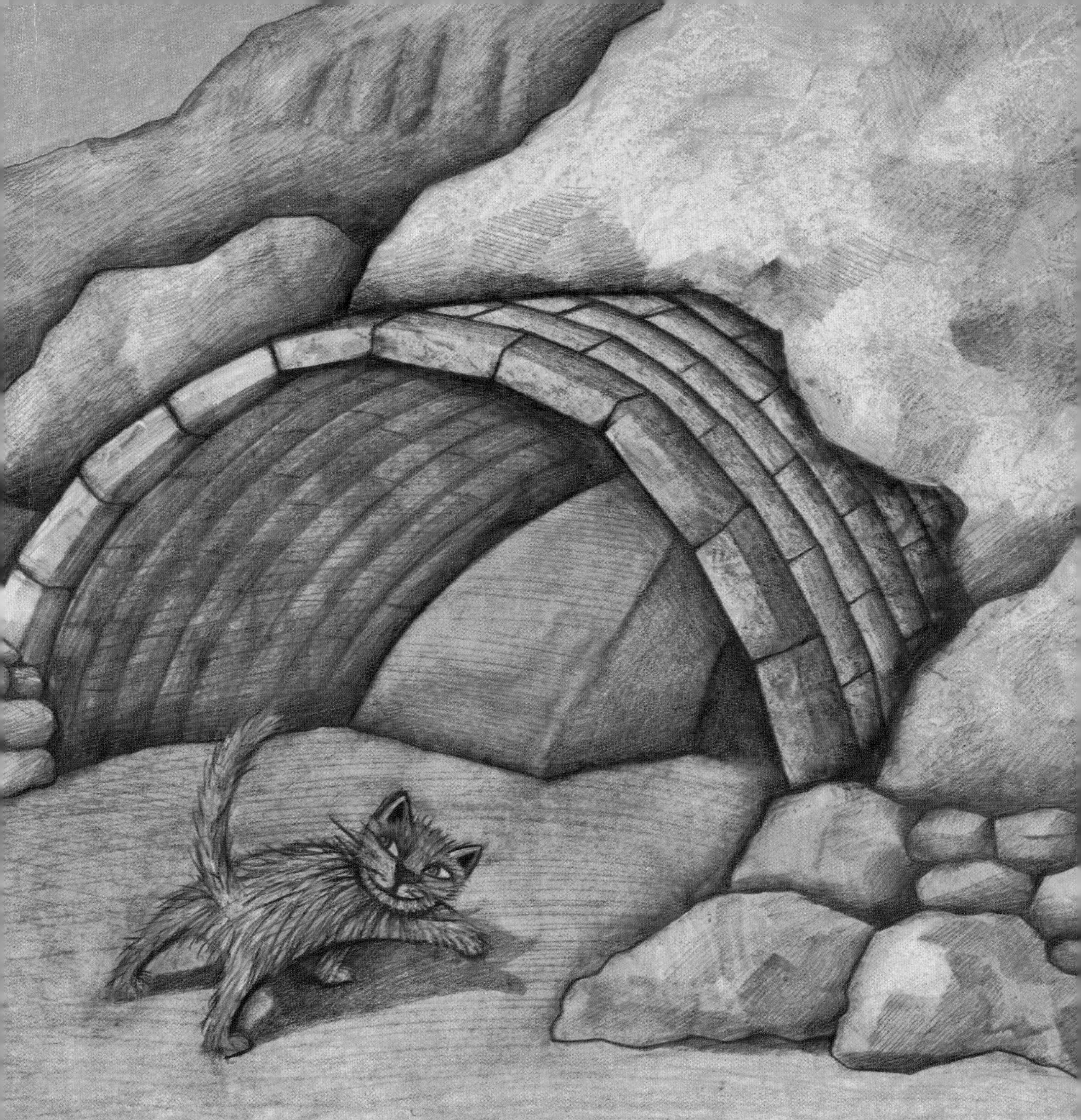

I adore cats, though I can't stroke them because I'm allergic to their fur. All the same, I crept away from the group to catch up with it and take its photo ...

Then, all of a sudden, it ran into a dark tunnel in the rock.

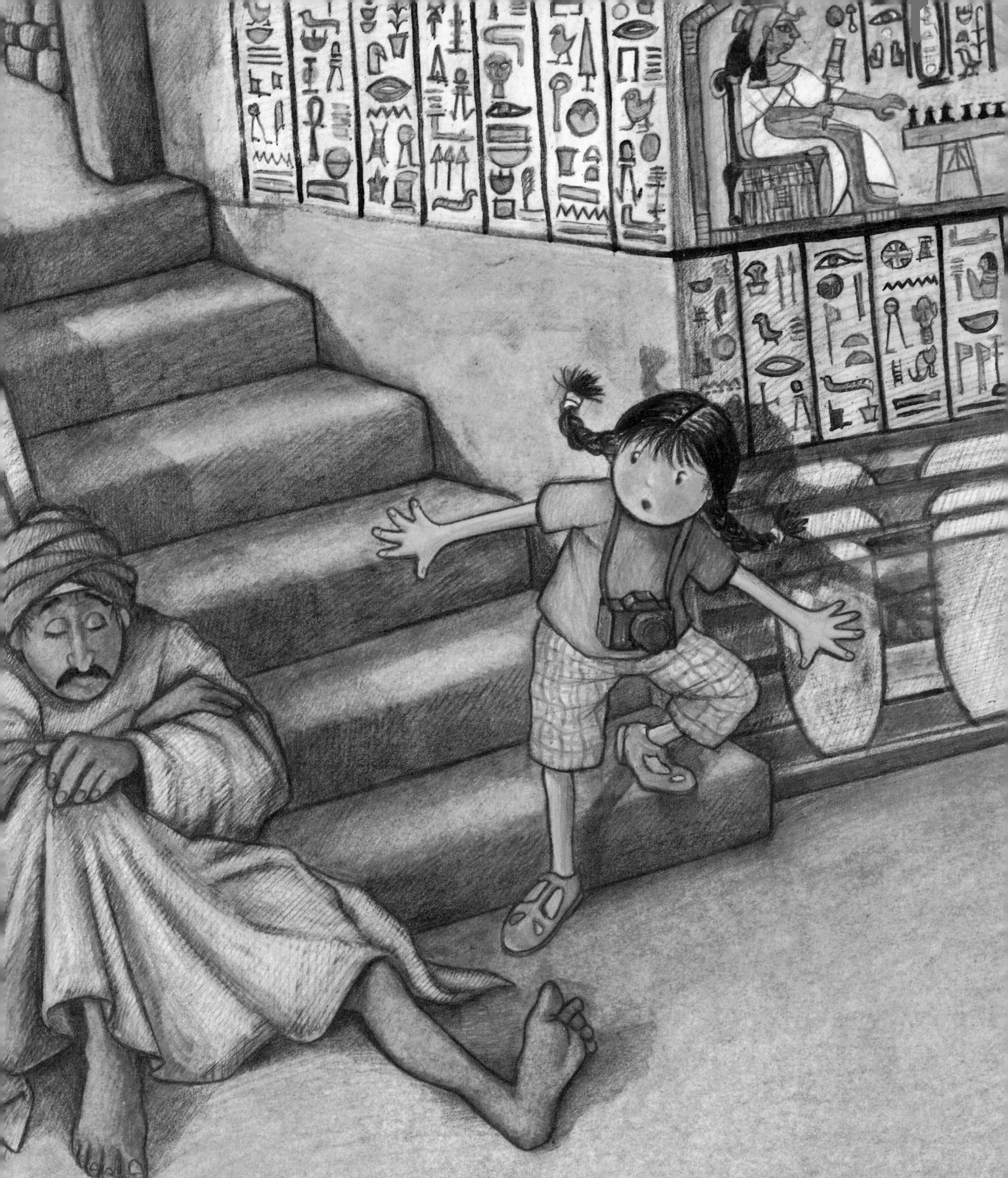

But when I went to look, I saw that it wasn't a tunnel – it was the entrance to an ancient tomb! Following the cat inside, I went down some steps and almost tripped over the tomb guard, who was fast asleep at the bottom.

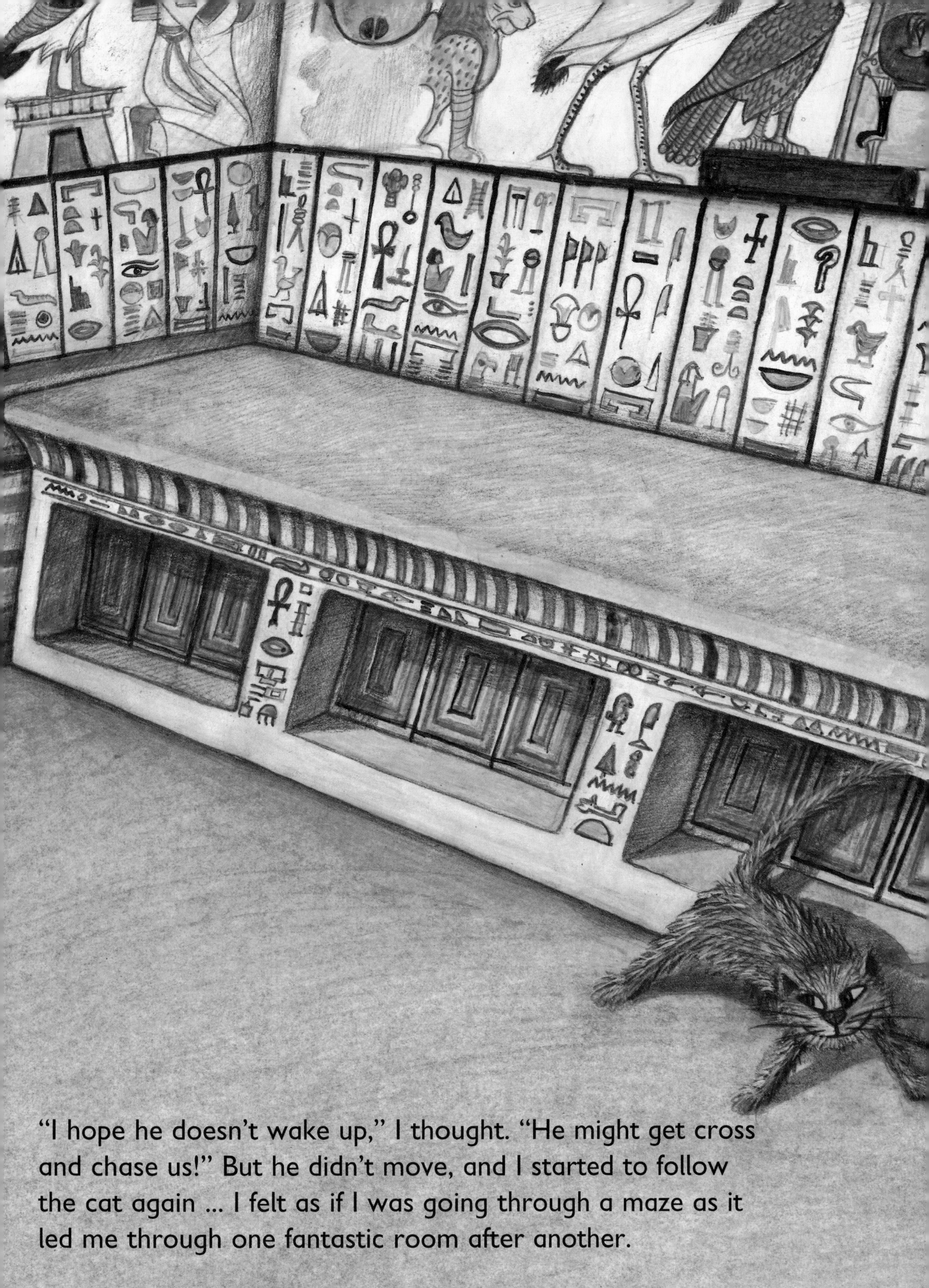

"I hope he doesn't wake up," I thought. "He might get cross and chase us!" But he didn't move, and I started to follow the cat again ... I felt as if I was going through a maze as it led me through one fantastic room after another.

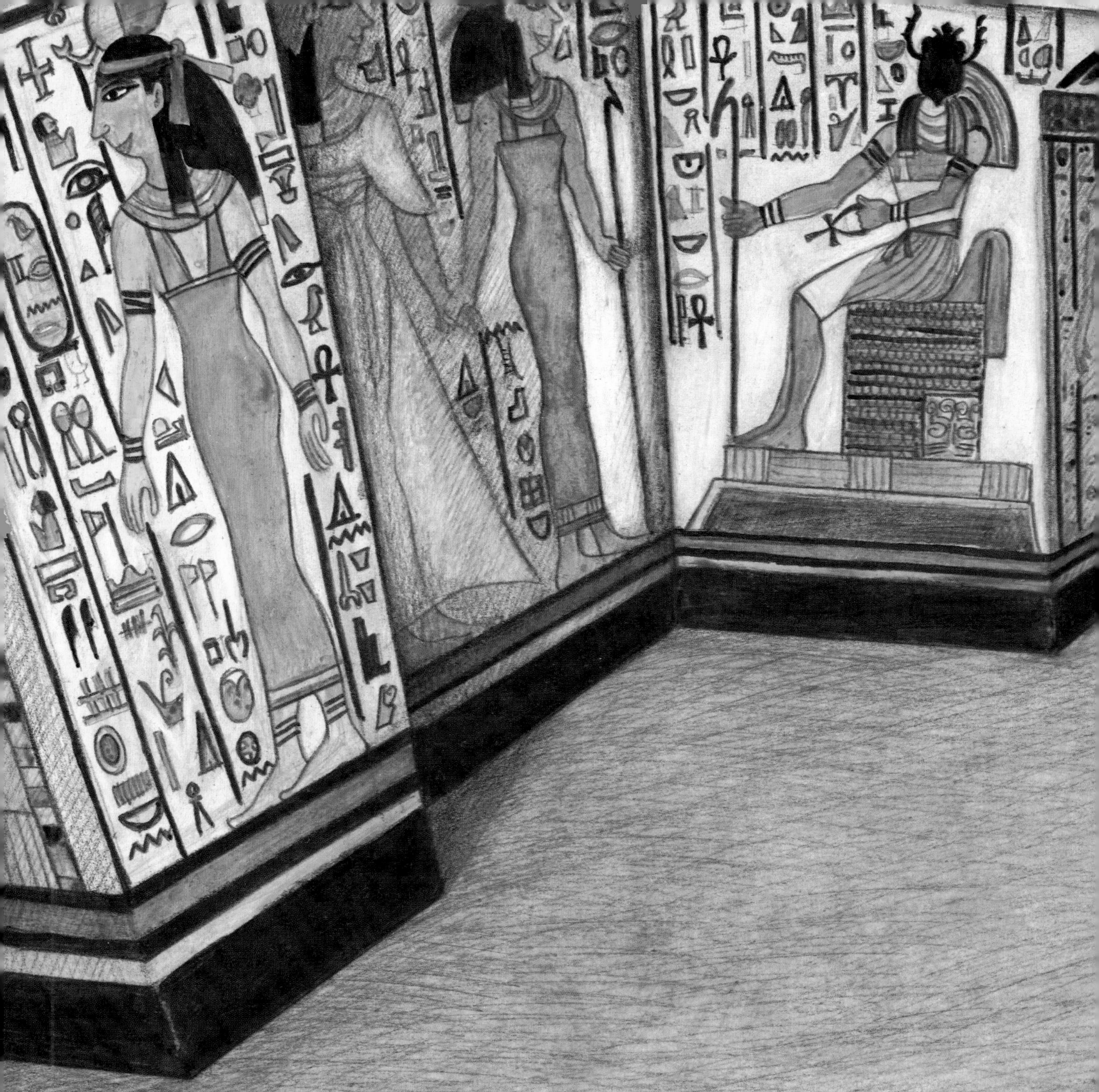

The ceilings were painted like skies dotted with stars, and even the walls were decorated all over. There were pictures of people in fancy clothes, and animals, too, strange creatures and monsters – one was like a man with a beetle for a head!

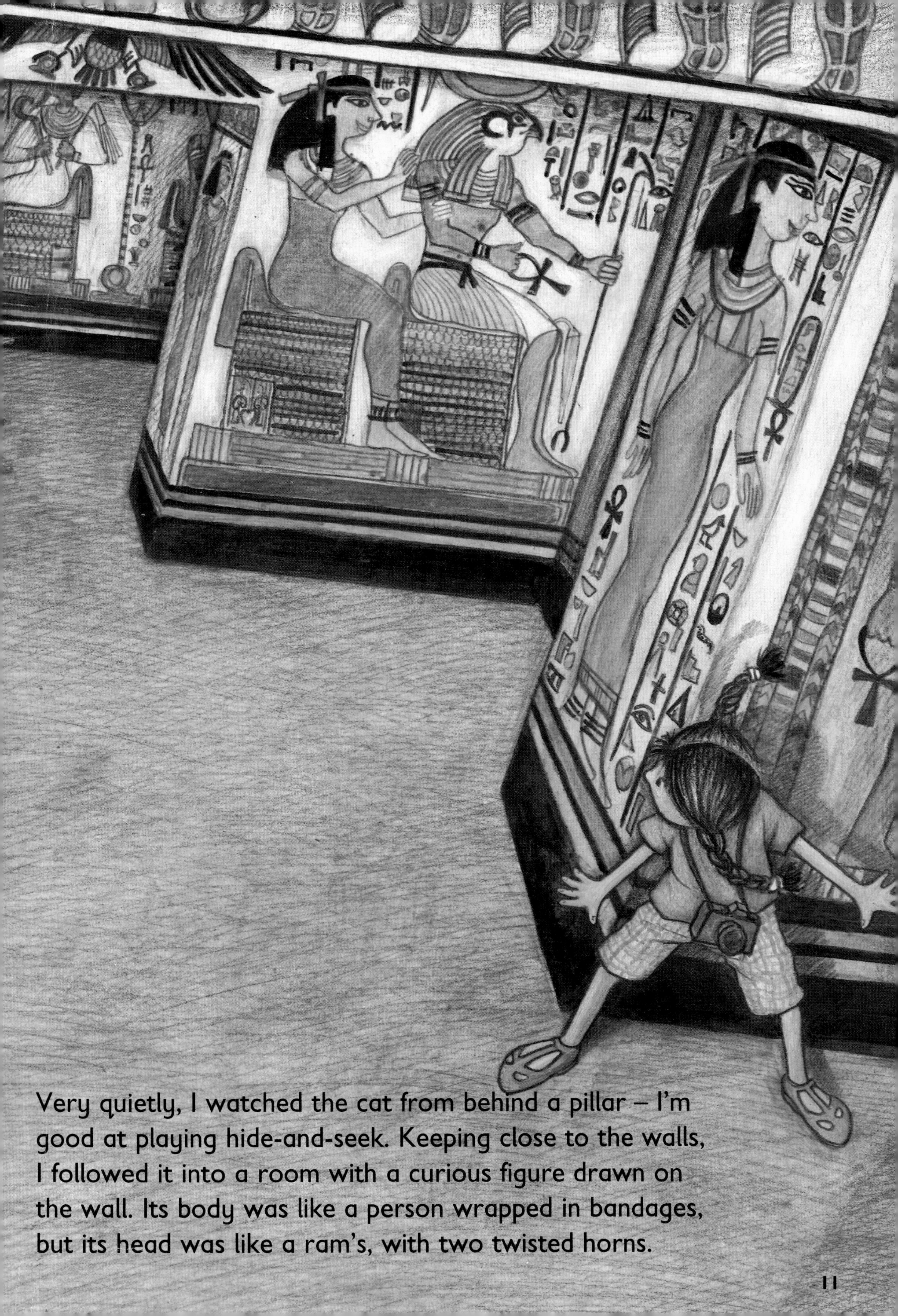

Very quietly, I watched the cat from behind a pillar – I'm good at playing hide-and-seek. Keeping close to the walls, I followed it into a room with a curious figure drawn on the wall. Its body was like a person wrapped in bandages, but its head was like a ram's, with two twisted horns.

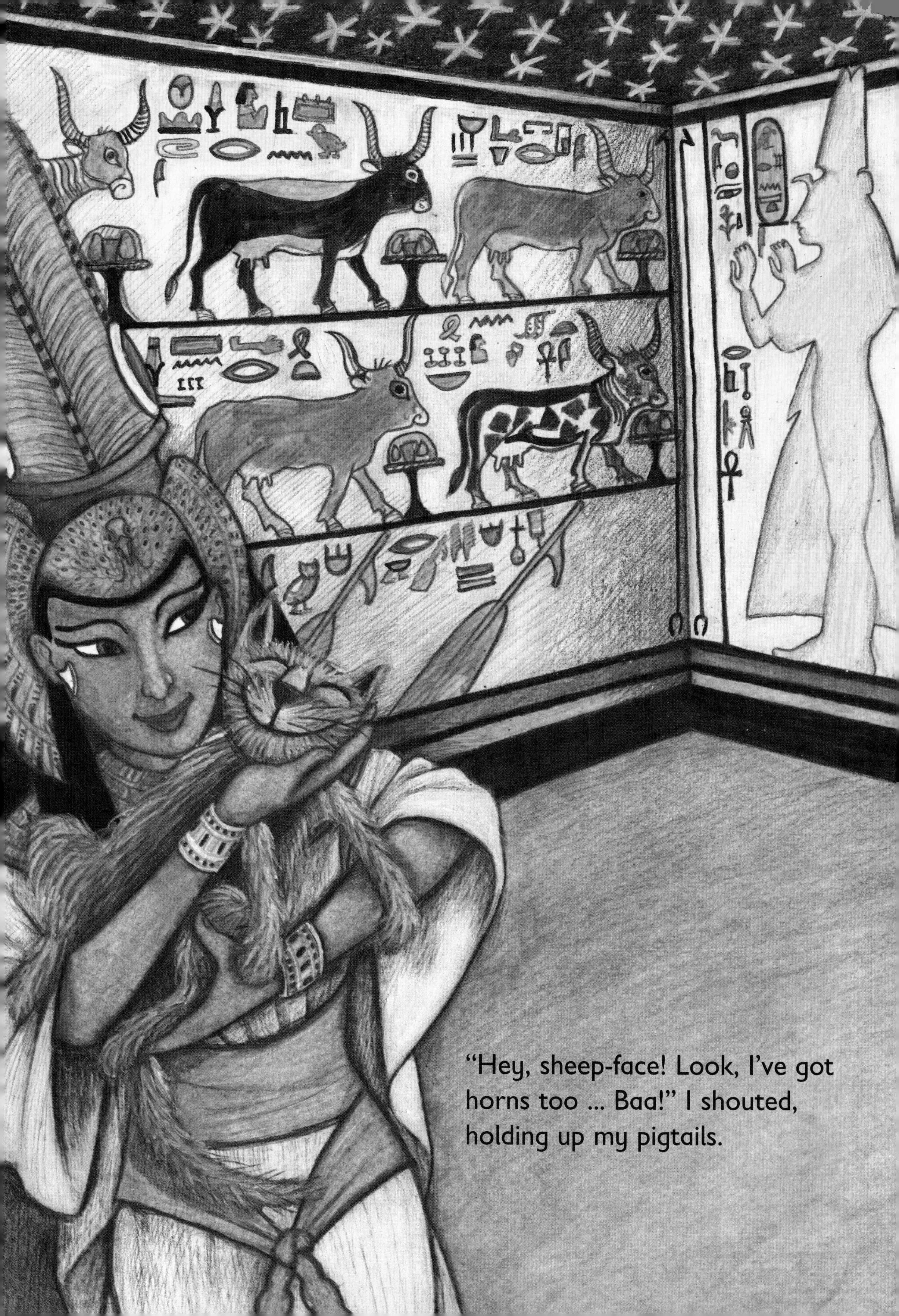

"Hey, sheep-face! Look, I've got horns too ... Baa!" I shouted, holding up my pigtails.

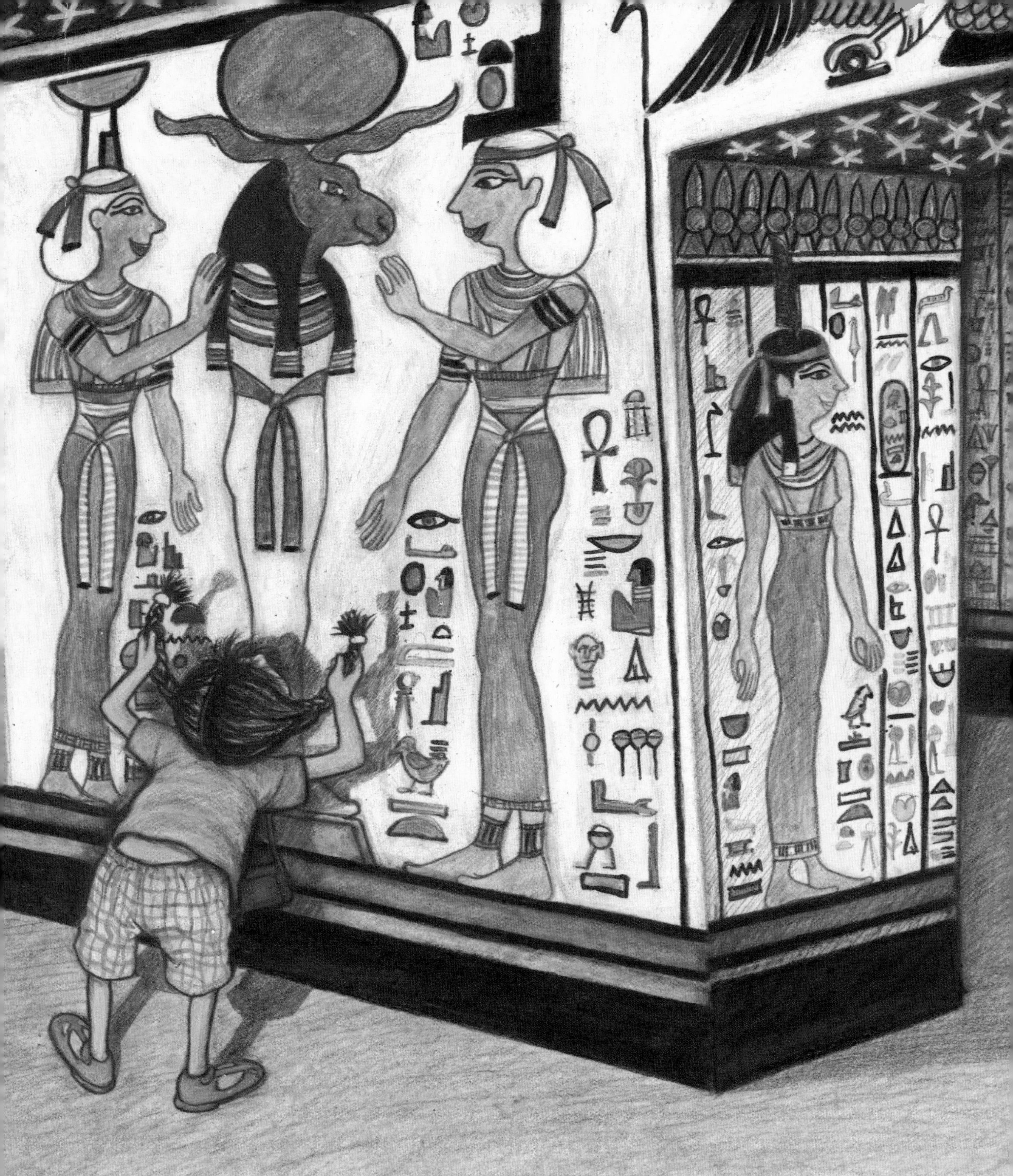

"That's not funny, little girl!" a voice behind me said. "It isn't nice to insult a god! Don't you recognize the great Osiris-Ra, sun god and lord of the Underworld? And this dear cat you've been chasing is important, too. Don't you know that cats are sacred in Egypt? Haven't you ever heard of the cat goddess Bastet, the daughter of Ra?"

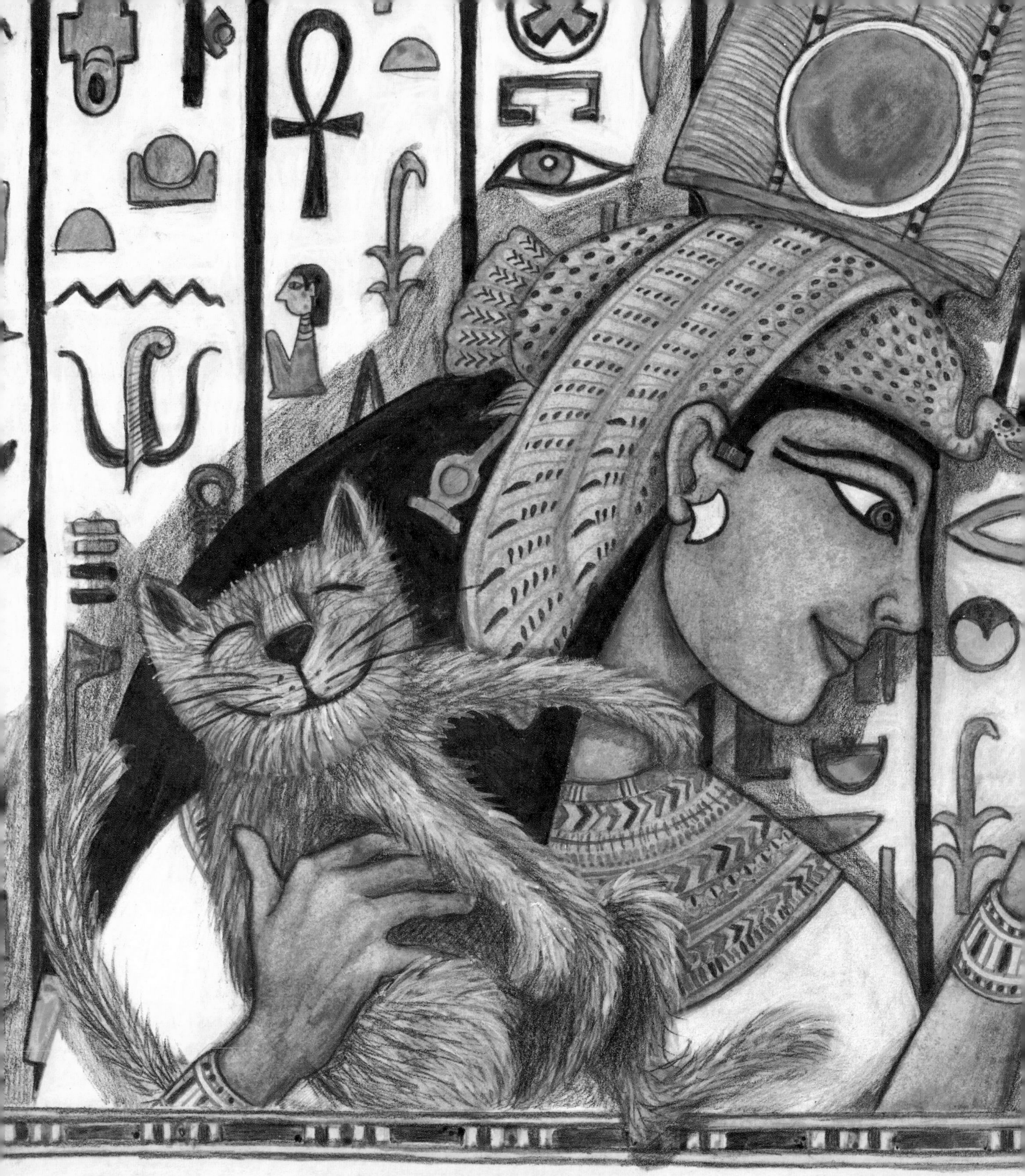

"No, never ... I only wanted to take a photo of her!"
I stared at the beautiful woman standing in front of me. She looked elegant and radiant, like a queen.
"*What* did you want to do to my cat?" she asked, holding it tightly in her arms.
"Oh, nothing bad!" I explained. "Look, this machine can

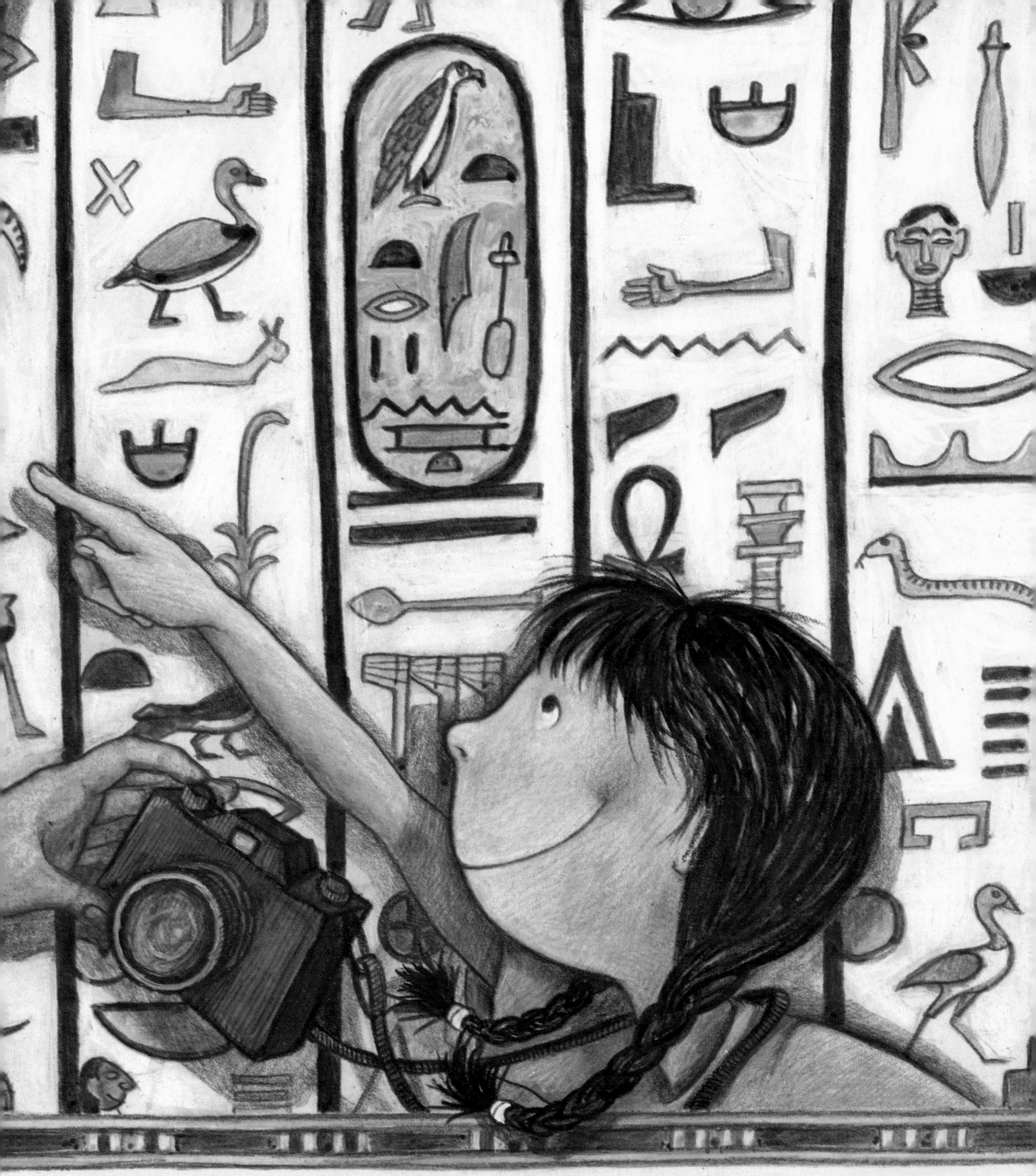

make pictures. All you have to do is this and ... *click* ... that's what we call a photo."

"Oh, how wonderful!" she cried, waving her arm at the walls. "In my day it took years to make pictures like these."

"Do you mean ...?" I began.

"Yes, little girl," she said proudly, "This is my tomb."

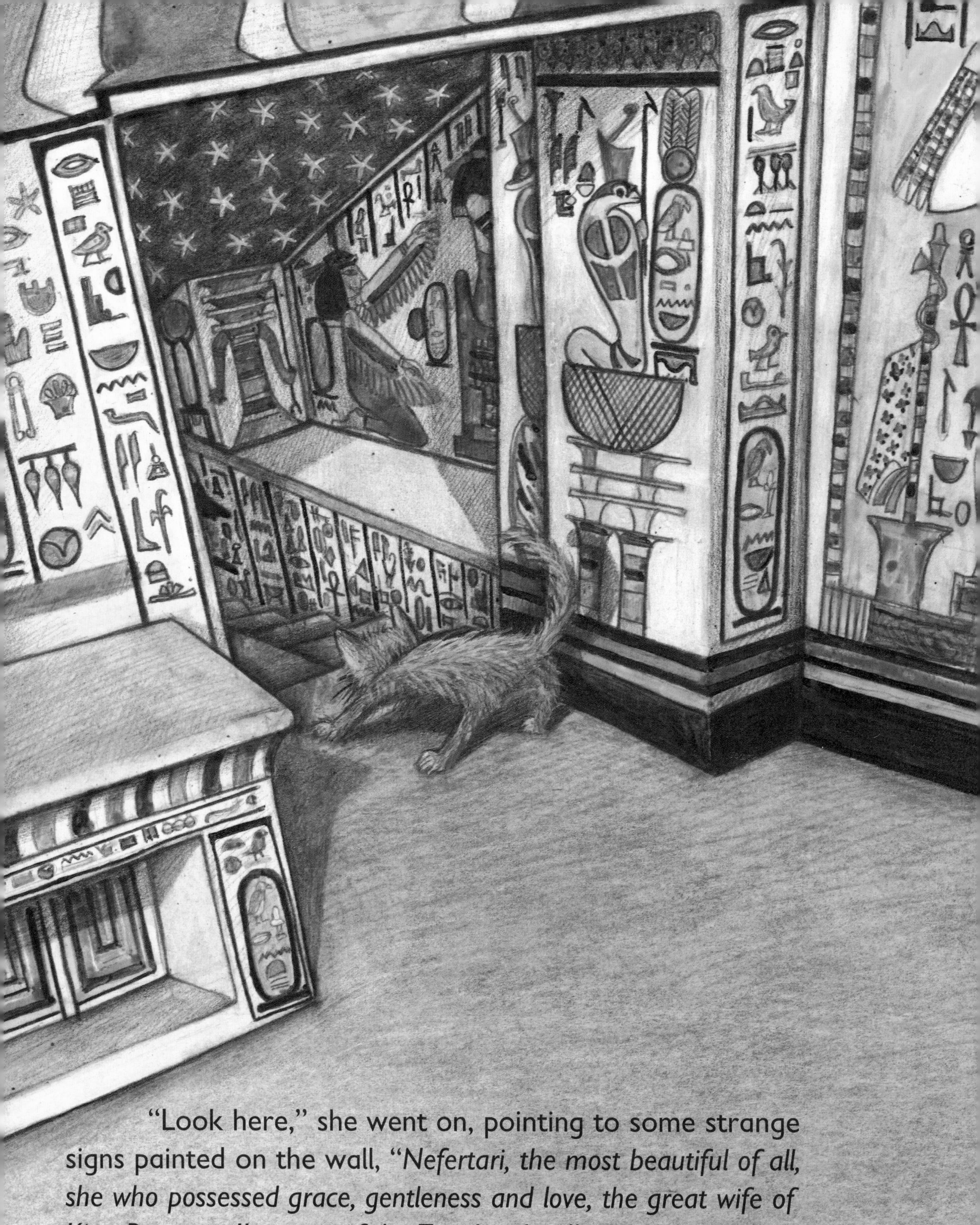

“Look here,” she went on, pointing to some strange signs painted on the wall, “*Nefertari, the most beautiful of all, she who possessed grace, gentleness and love, the great wife of King Rameses II, queen of the Two Lands ...*”

I couldn’t believe my eyes and ears. “Oh, Nefertari,” I gasped, “I believe you, but I don’t know how to read those strange signs.”

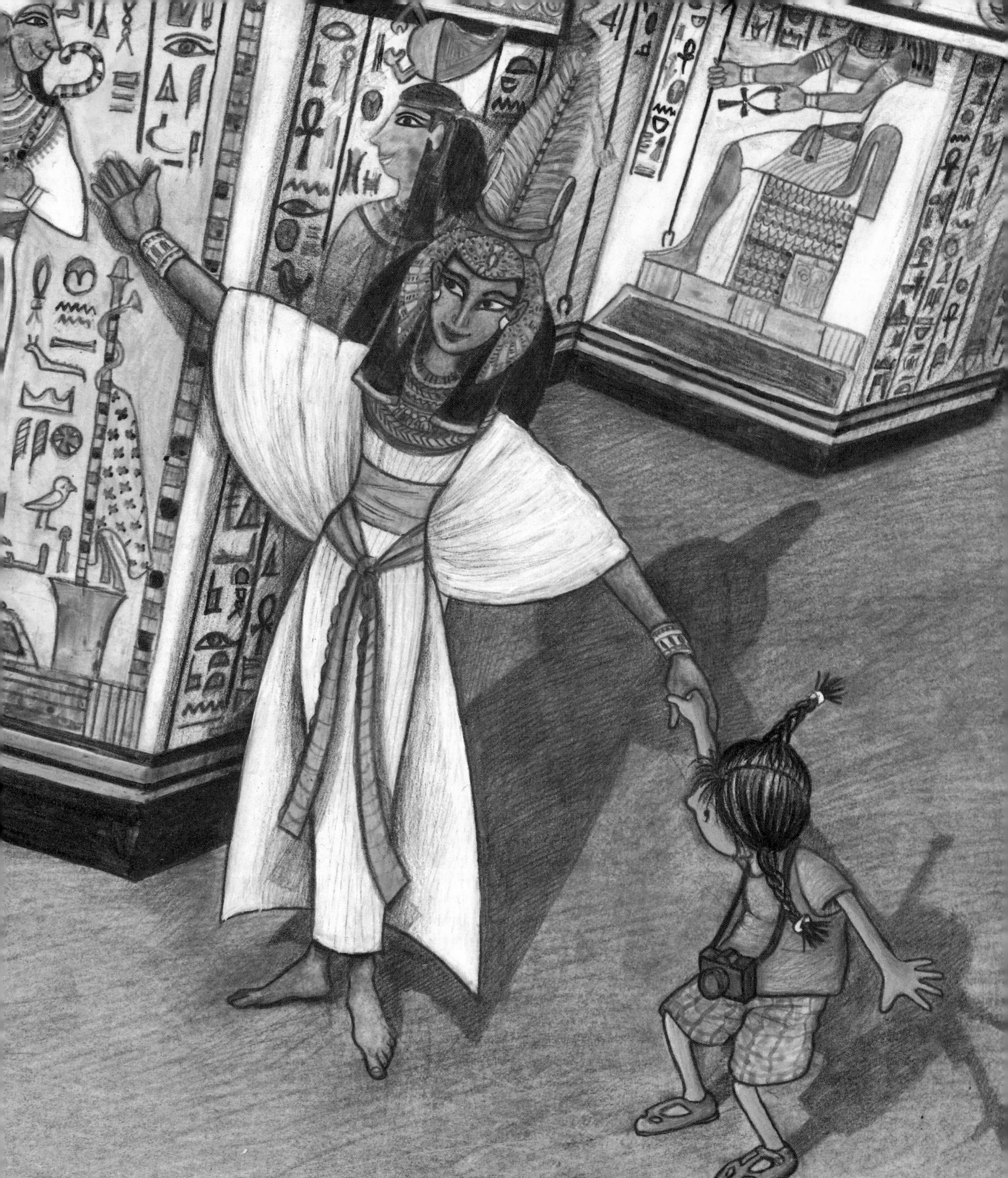

Nefertari looked surprised. “They’re called hieroglyphs, and we use them to write our language,” she explained. “You don’t seem to be a very well-educated girl! Well then, it’s up to me to be your teacher.” Nefertari took me by the hand and started to explain many of the interesting and mysterious things around us.

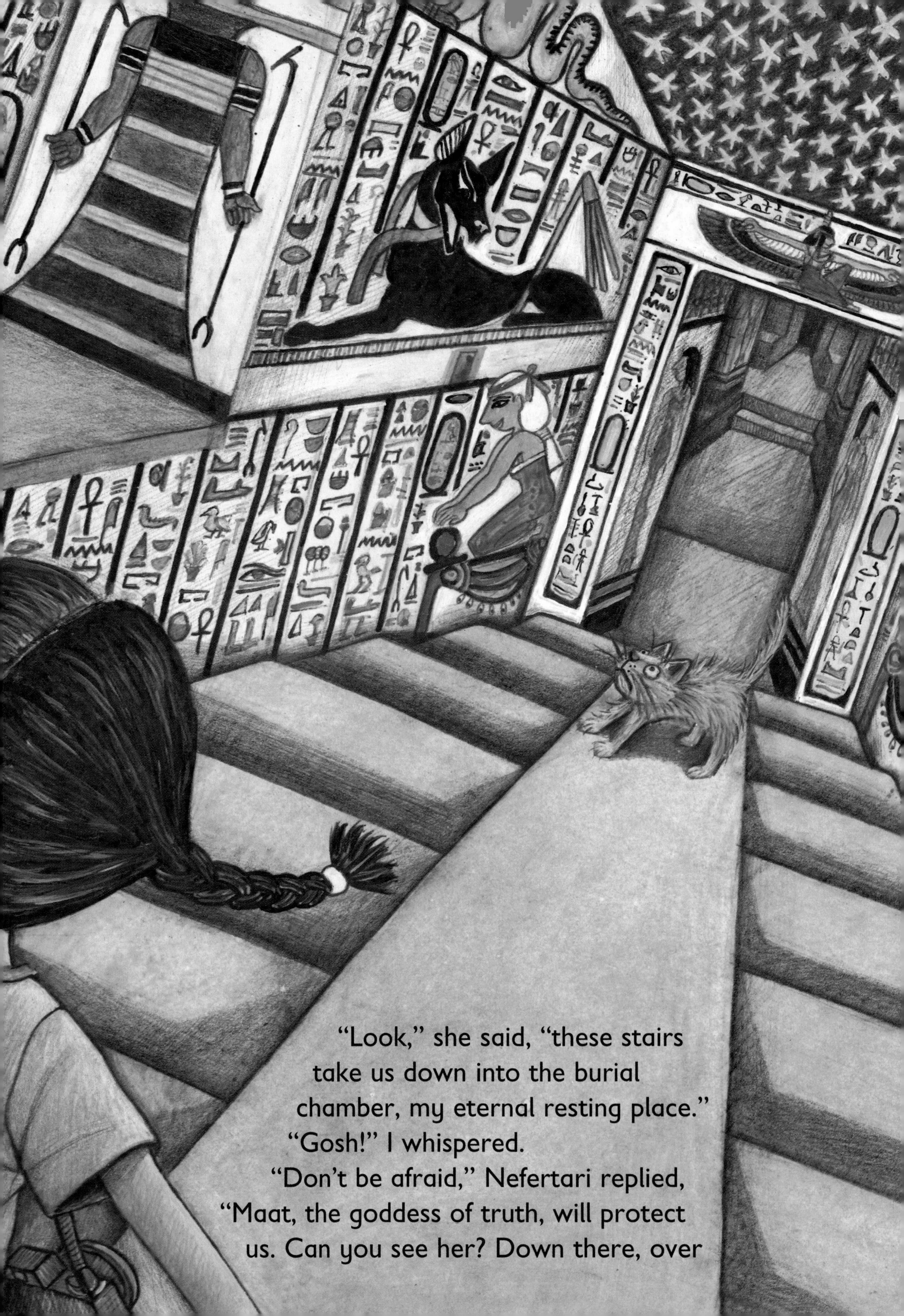

“Look,” she said, “these stairs take us down into the burial chamber, my eternal resting place.”

“Gosh!” I whispered.

“Don’t be afraid,” Nefertari replied, “Maat, the goddess of truth, will protect us. Can you see her? Down there, over

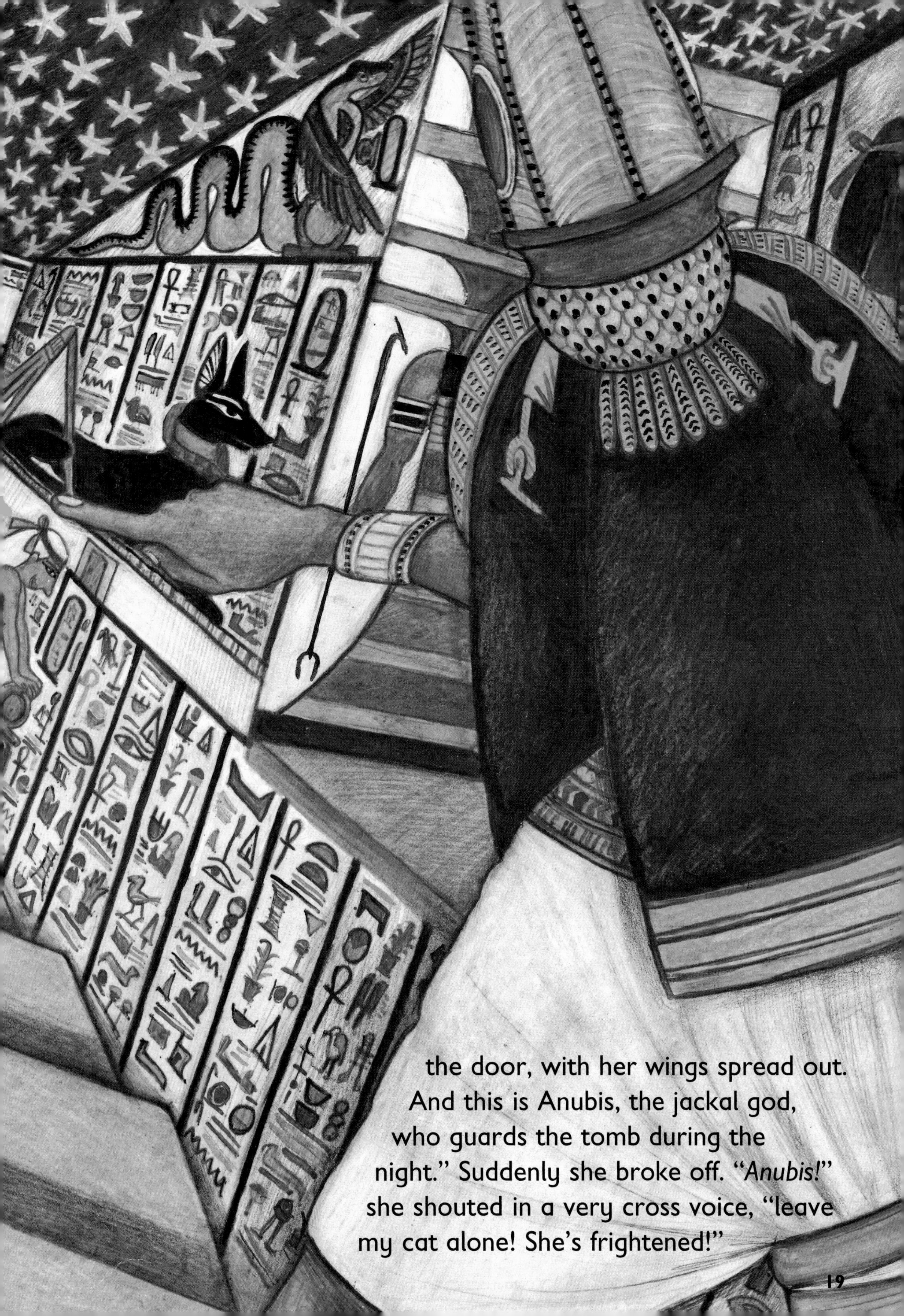

the door, with her wings spread out. And this is Anubis, the jackal god, who guards the tomb during the night." Suddenly she broke off. "*Anubis!*" she shouted in a very cross voice, "leave my cat alone! She's frightened!"

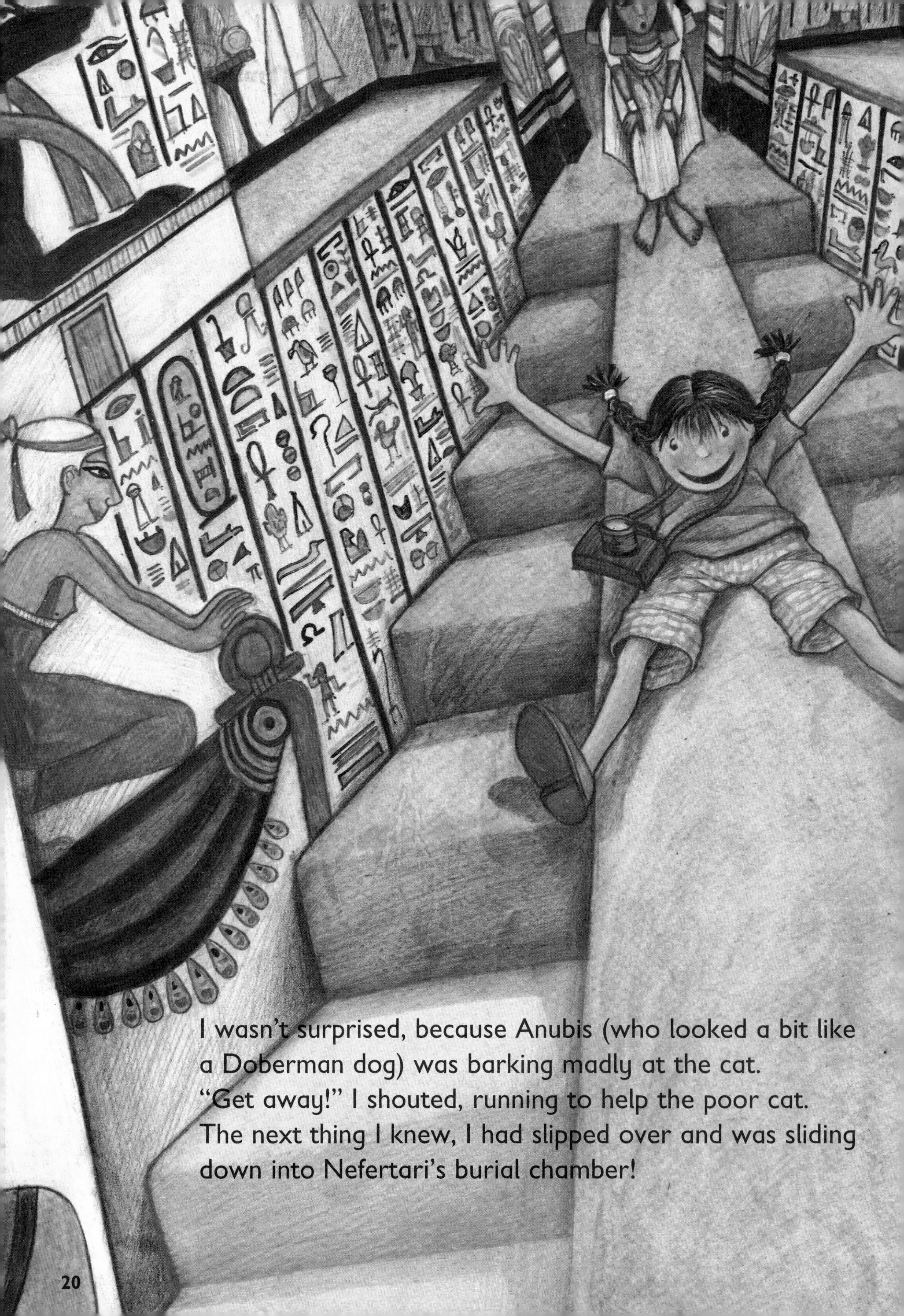

I wasn't surprised, because Anubis (who looked a bit like a Doberman dog) was barking madly at the cat.
"Get away!" I shouted, running to help the poor cat.
The next thing I knew, I had slipped over and was sliding down into Nefertari's burial chamber!

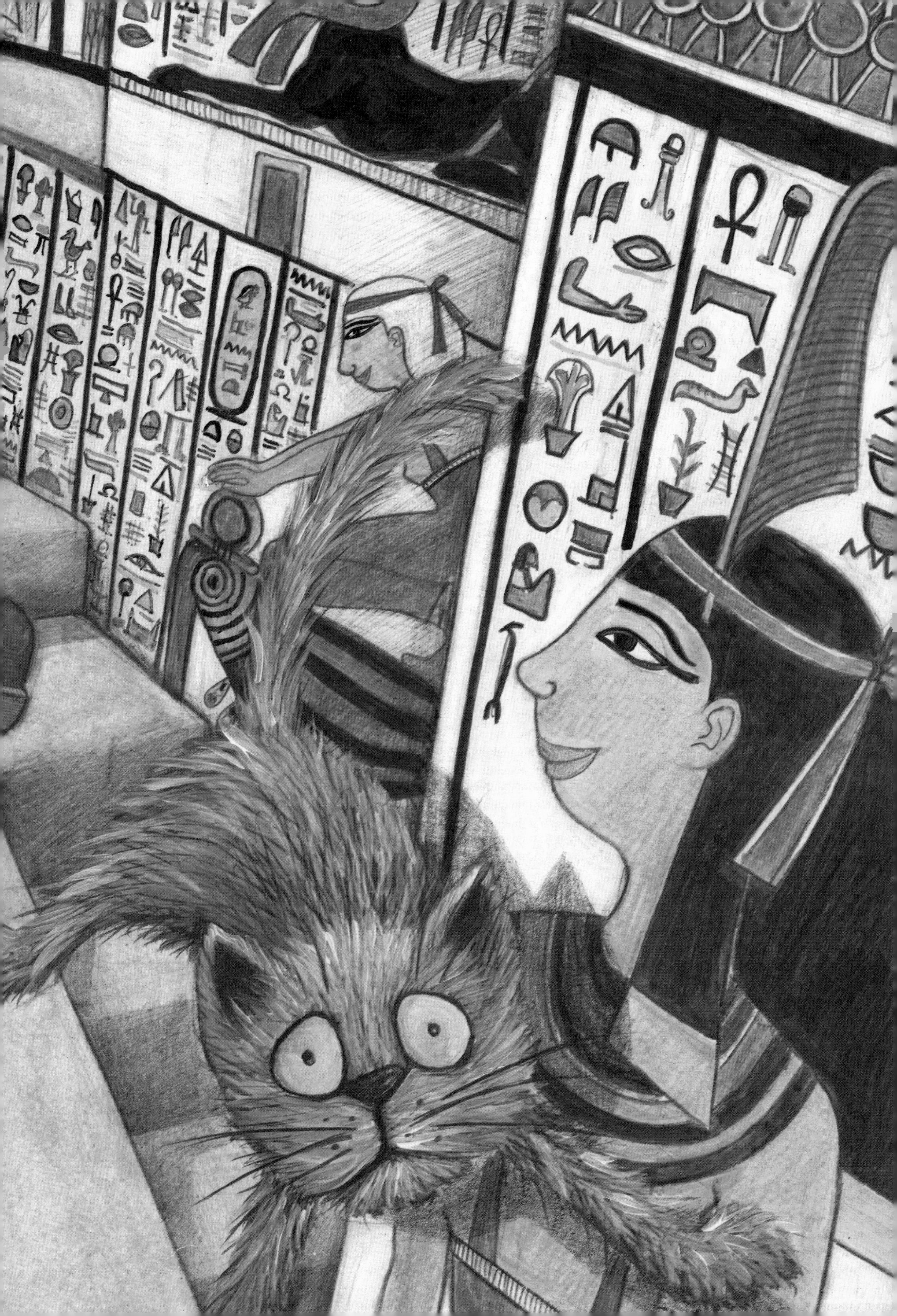

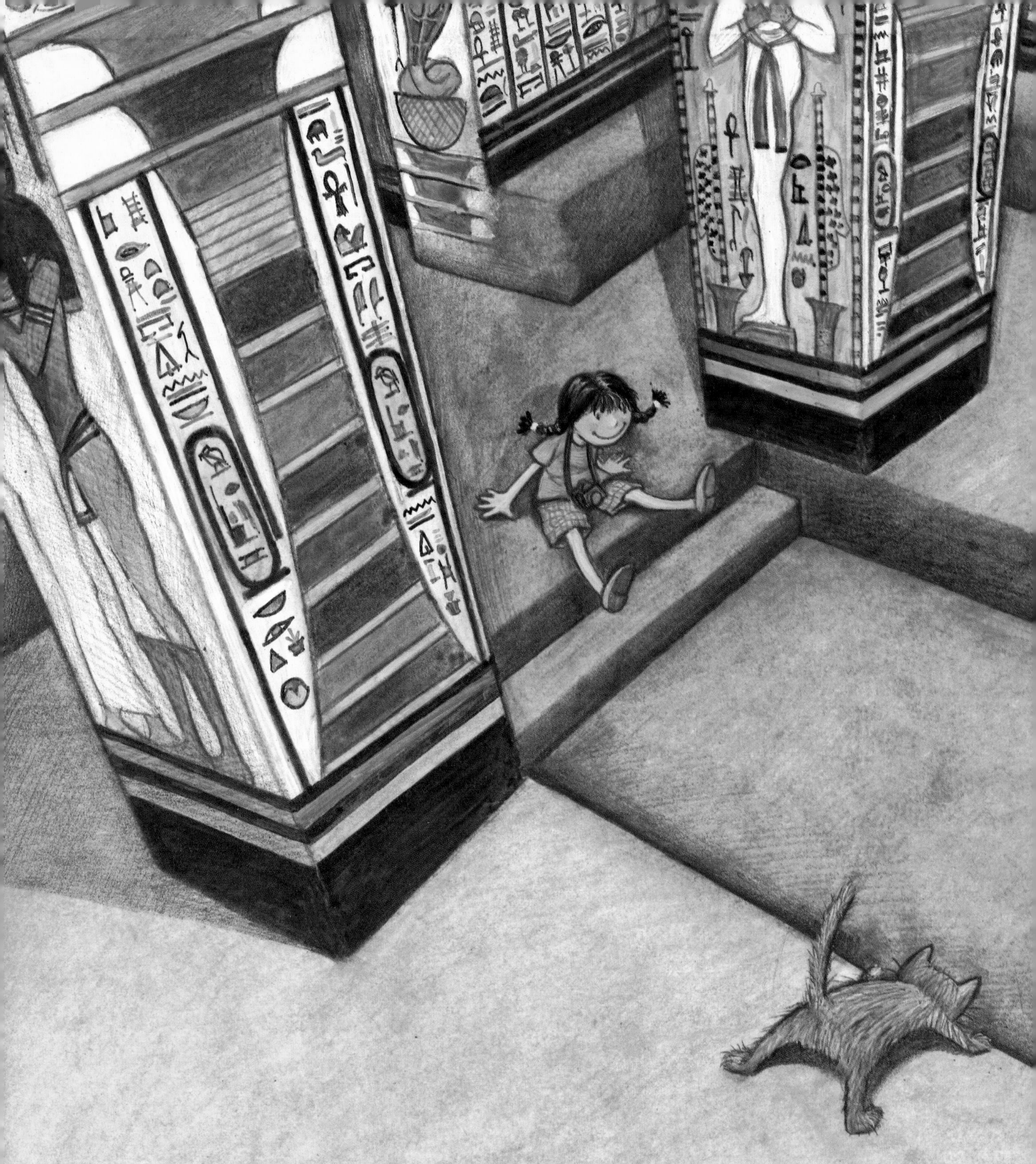

I looked around, wondering where the sarcophagus was. I knew from the other tombs we'd seen that there ought to be one, but here there was only a big hole in the ground.

"You'll have to imagine my sarcophagus," said Nefertari, as if she had read my mind. "It had a lovely pink granite cover, and around it were all my precious things – jars of perfume, caskets, jewels – but people came and took nearly everything away."

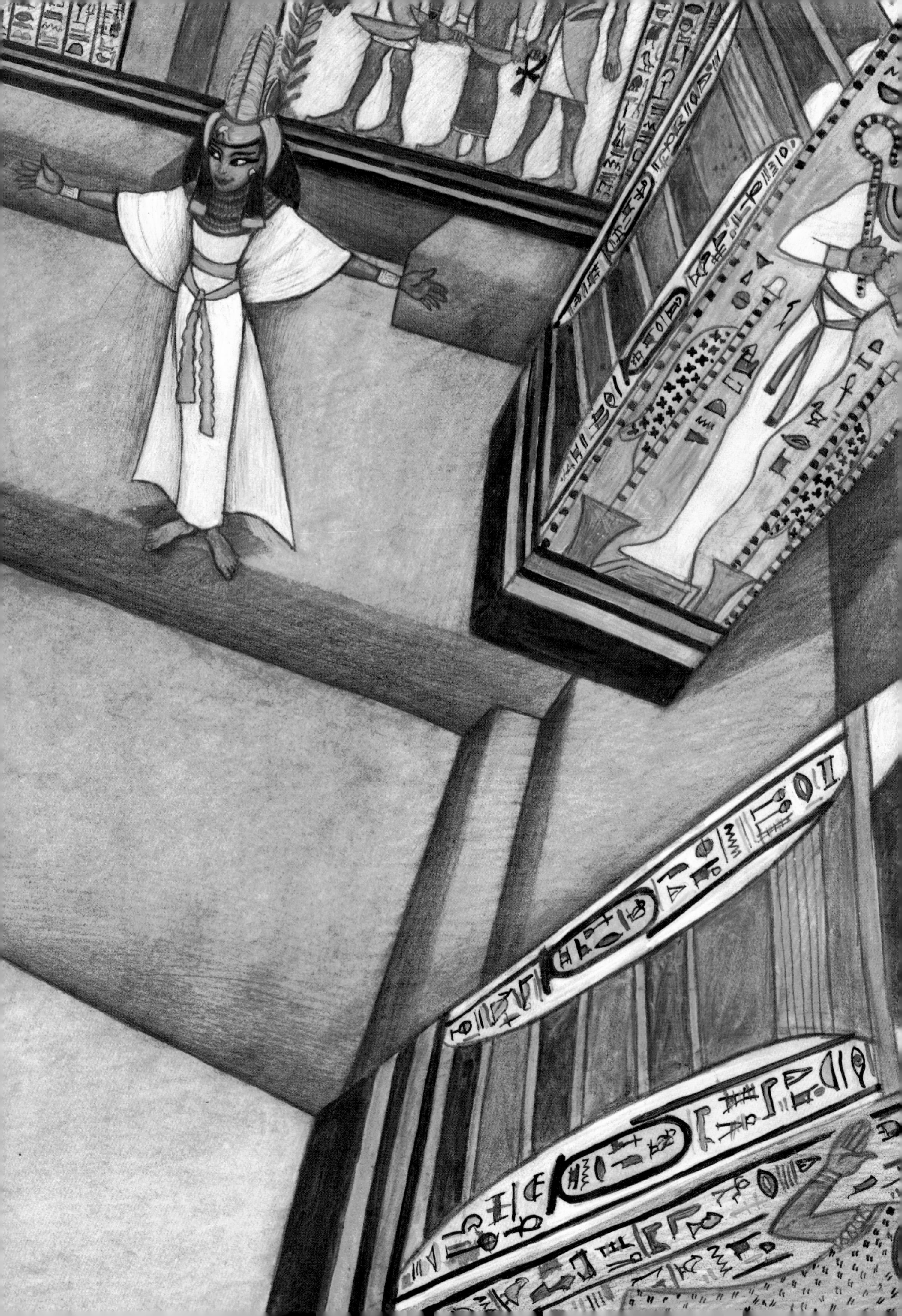

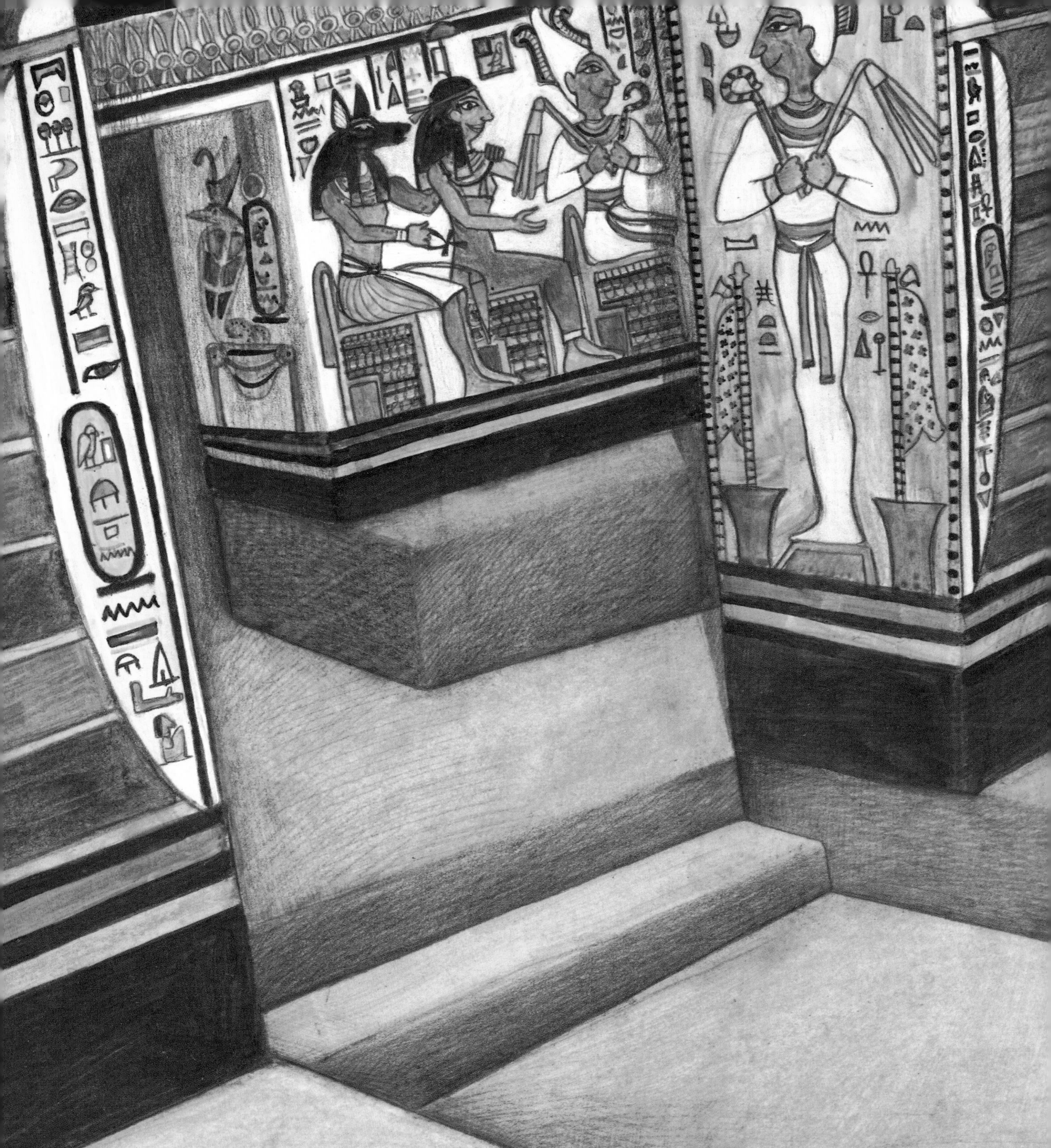

"Never mind," she went on, "I have an idea ... Could you use your machine to make a picture of us all together?"

"Of course!" I replied, "It would be a lovely souvenir!"

"Good," said Nefertari, "then I'll go and settle myself down over there with my dear Anubis and Osiris-Ra." I was so excited at the idea of being in a photo with Nefertari and the gods that I didn't notice the cat was right under my nose ... until it was too late ...

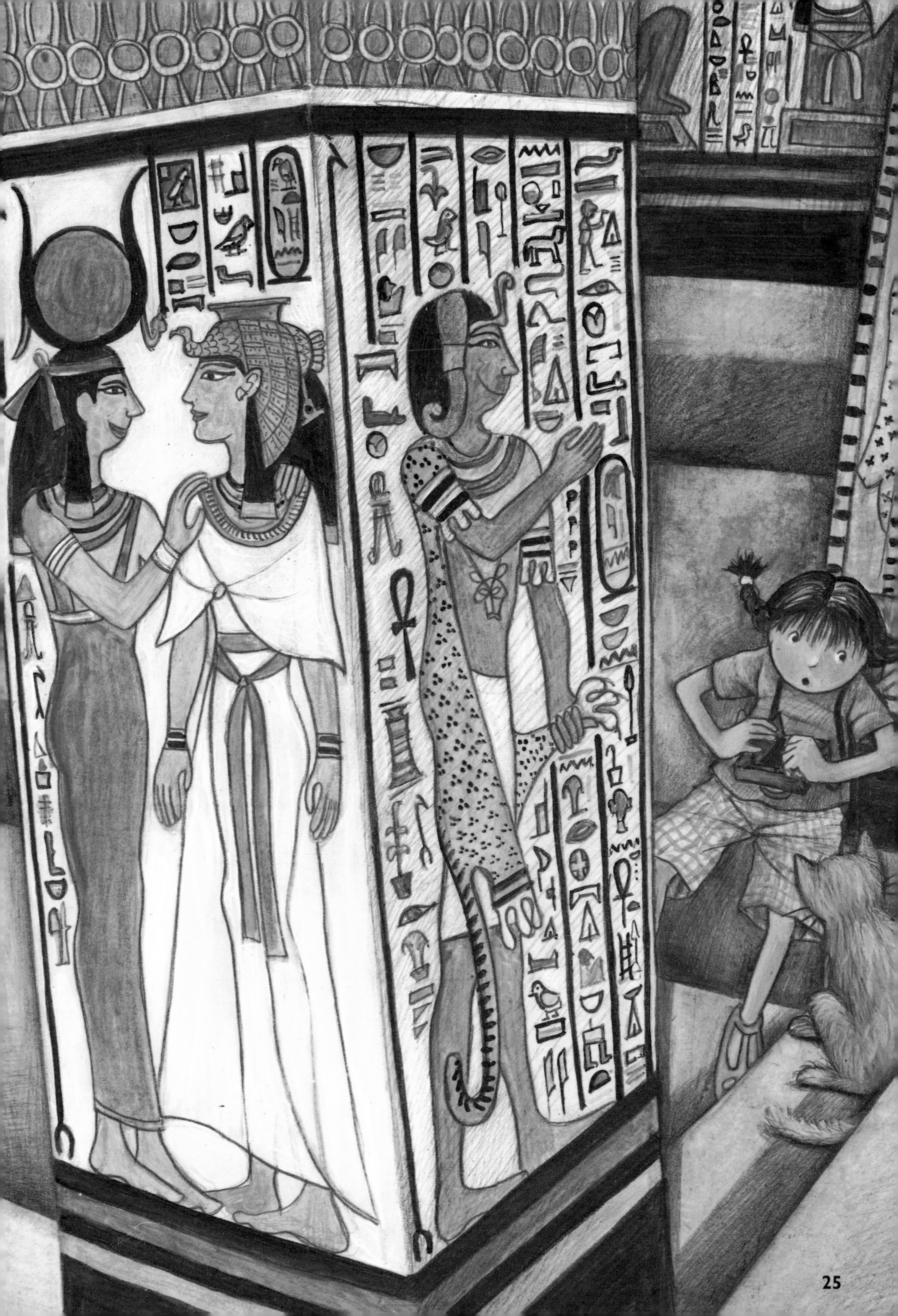

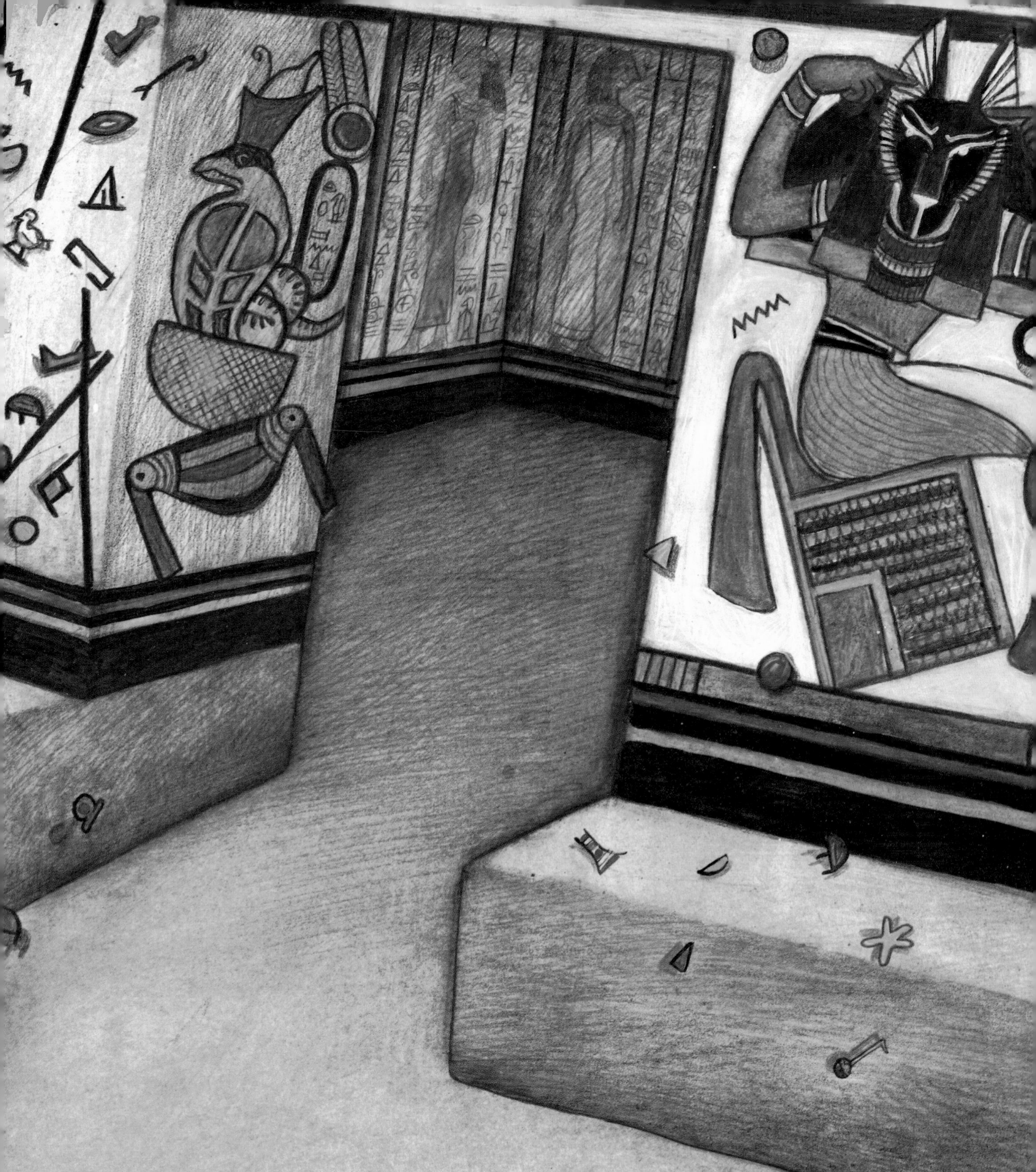

"Oh no! Please, pussycat, don't come too close! You're very nice, but I'm ... *atchoo!* ... allergic to cats!"

And out came a huge sneeze that seemed to shake the whole room! Stars and hieroglyphs tumbled onto the ground, all the paintings fell apart ... and when it was all over, everyone had vanished.

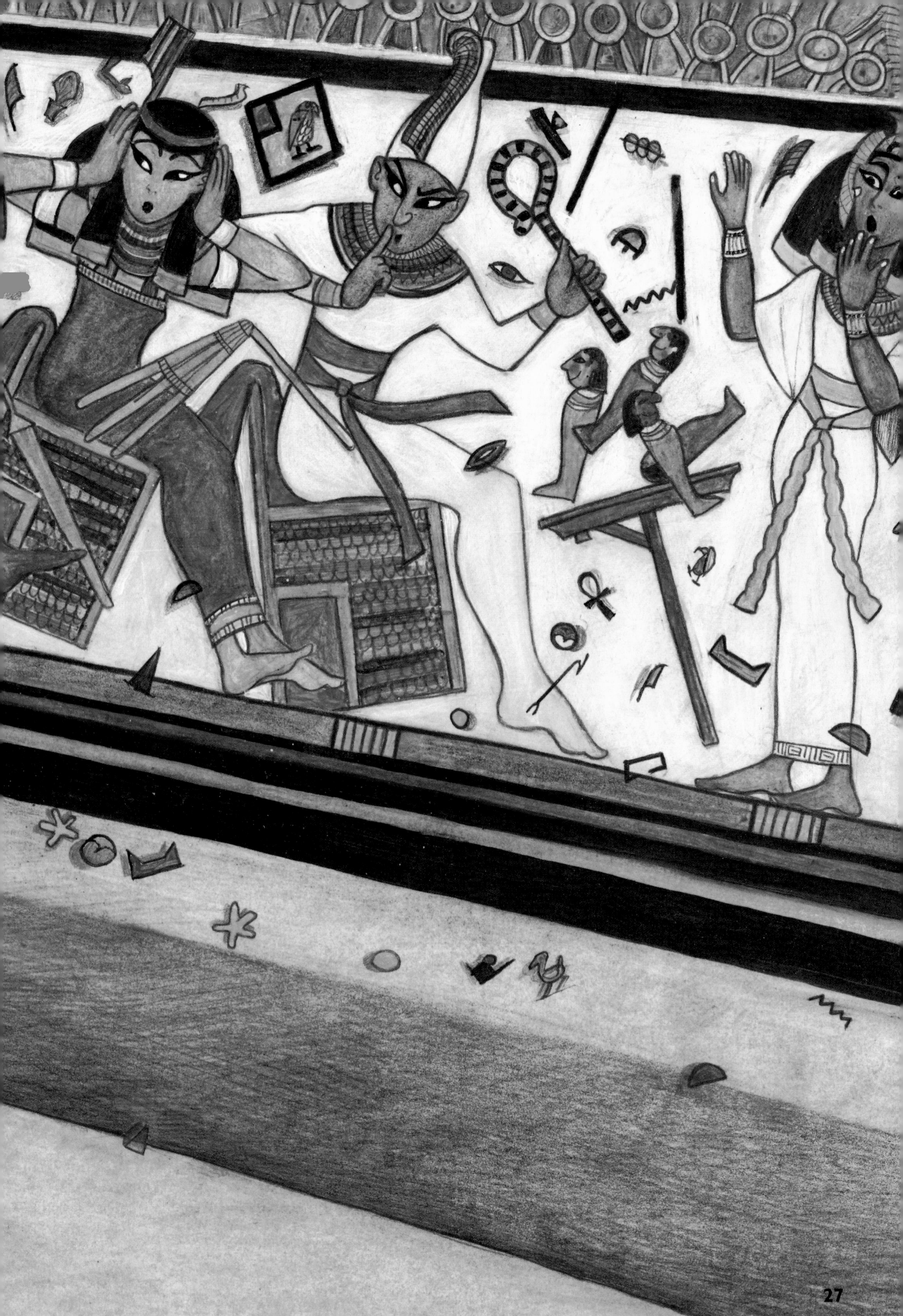

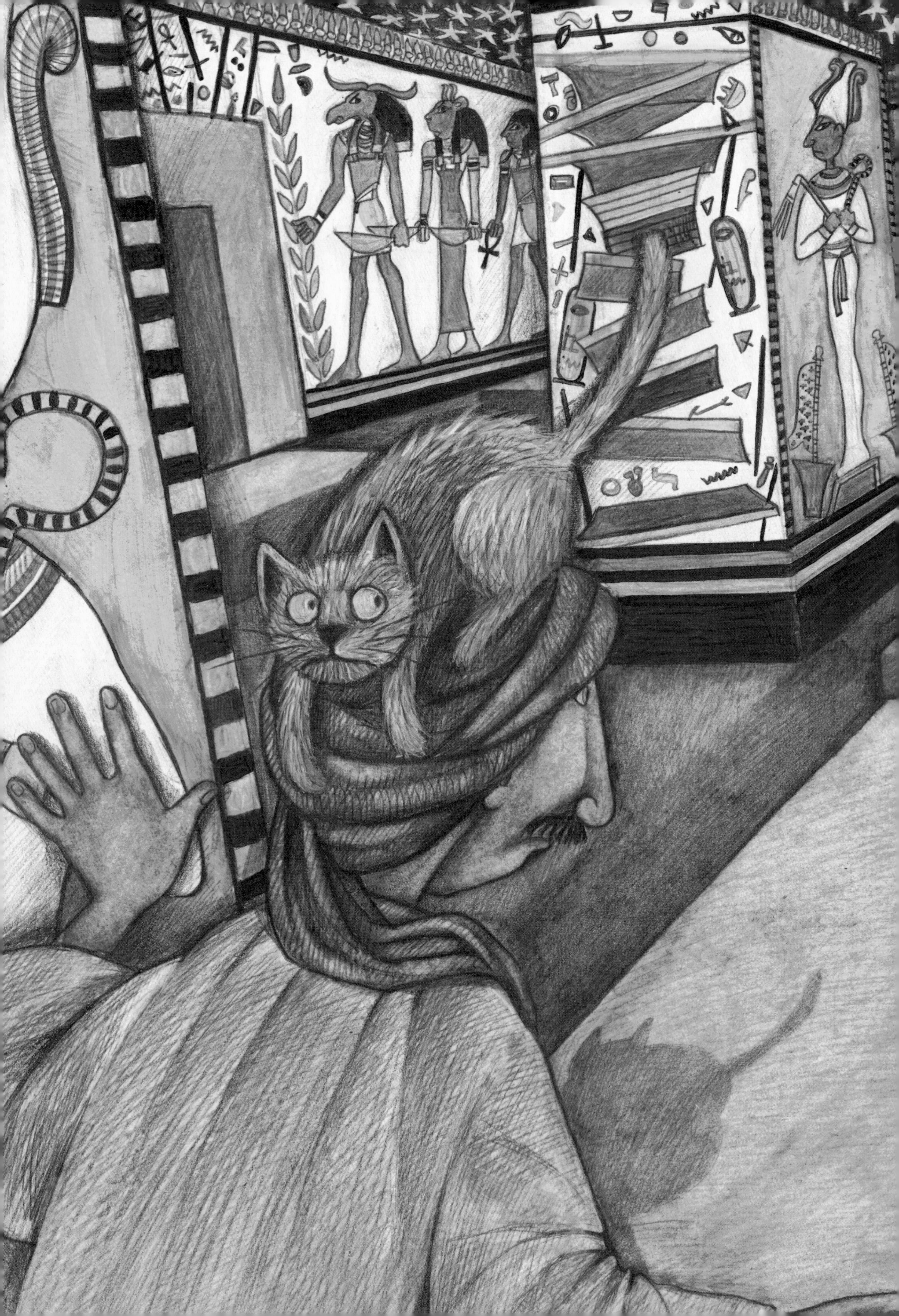

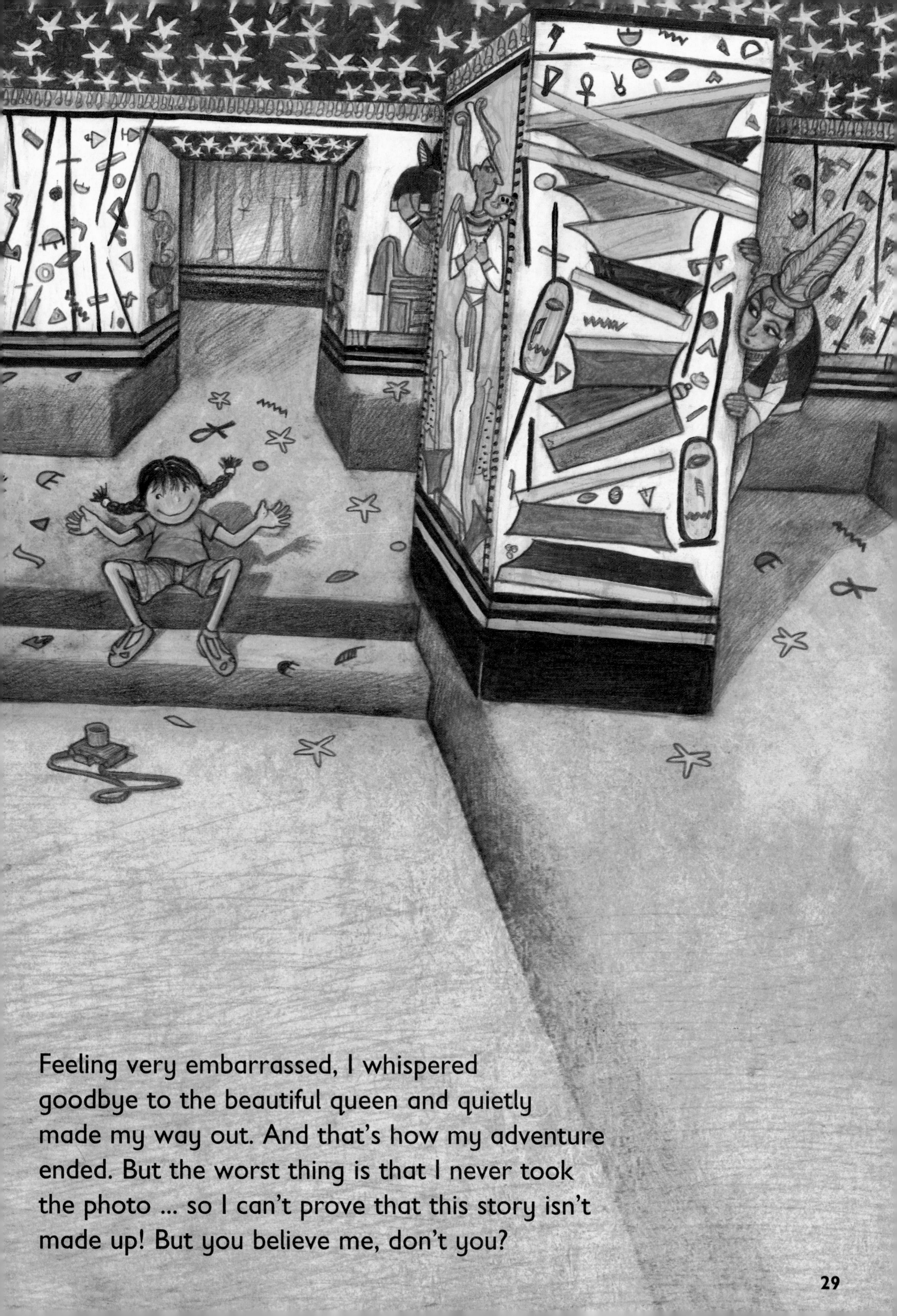

Feeling very embarrassed, I whispered goodbye to the beautiful queen and quietly made my way out. And that's how my adventure ended. But the worst thing is that I never took the photo ... so I can't prove that this story isn't made up! But you believe me, don't you?

WHO WERE THE EGYPTIANS?

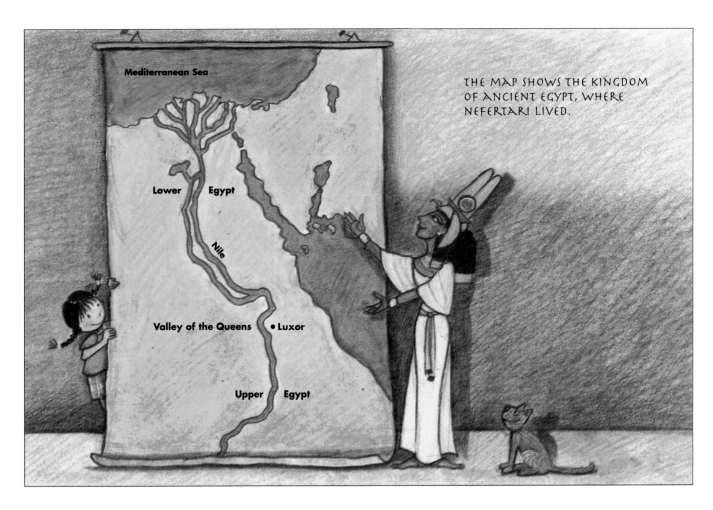

Mediterranean Sea
Lower Egypt
Nile
Valley of the Queens
Luxor
Upper Egypt
THE MAP SHOWS THE KINGDOM OF ANCIENT EGYPT, WHERE NEFERTARI LIVED.

THE EGYPTIAN CIVILIZATION WAS ONE OF THE OLDEST AND MOST REFINED IN THE WORLD.
ITS GREATEST SPLENDOR WAS IN THE TIME OF THE PHARAOHS, BETWEEN 3000 BC AND 525 BC, WHEN EGYPT FELL TO THE PERSIANS. THE KINGDOM OF EGYPT STRETCHED FROM NUBIA IN MODERN SUDAN TO THE NILE DELTA; MOST OF ITS TERRITORY WAS MADE UP OF DESERT, KNOWN AS THE RED LAND.

THE EGYPTIANS WERE FARMERS WHO LIVED ALONG THE BANKS OF THE RIVER NILE. THIS AREA WAS CALLED THE BLACK LAND, BECAUSE OF THE PRECIOUS LAYER OF MUD THAT COVERED IT AFTER THE ANNUAL NILE FLOOD. WITHOUT THIS FERTILE LAND FOR GROWING FOOD, THERE COULD NEVER HAVE BEEN A CIVILIZATION IN EGYPT.

• At the top of ancient Egyptian society was the king or **pharaoh**, who was the religious, political and military leader of Egypt. He was worshipped as a god, and his people believed that everything – the fortunes of the country, the growth of the crops, the flooding of the Nile and the healing of illnesses – depended on him. His power and wealth were invested in building temples, palaces and pyramids.

The pharaohs were surrounded by many officials. The most important of them was the **vizier**, who was responsible for collecting taxes and directing public works. The **priests**, who were very powerful and influential, celebrated

religious rites and enjoyed many privileges. **Scribes** were well-educated officials who were expert in writing and mathematical calculations and did much of the work of government. Below them, there were **soldiers** and **craftsmen**, **traders** and **peasants**, who had to work very hard. But the hardest work in the worst conditions, such as quarrying stone and building pyramids, was **forced labor**, often done by prisoners.

• By preserving their bodies after death, the Egyptians believed that they would live forever. This process, called **mummification**, involved removing the internal organs. The intestines, the stomach, the lungs and the liver were dried, wrapped in linen bandages and placed in

special vases called **canopic jars**, while the heart and the kidneys were left in the empty and dried-out body. At this point, the body was ready to be wrapped in linen bandages and placed in a coffin or a stone **sarcophagus**. The Egyptians believed that after death the soul left the body to meet **Osiris**, the

god who ruled the Underworld, and to be judged by him. Food and drink, clothes, and models of servants were placed near the sarcophagus to accompany the dead into the afterlife.

• Ancient Egyptian writing was very complicated and only trained scribes could use it. It was made up of about 700 picture signs called **hieroglyphs**, which could be written from right to left, from left to right or from top to bottom. They were written on monuments – such as tombs and temples – and on a kind of paper called **papyrus**.

• Egyptian religious buildings included **pyramids**, **temples** and **obelisks**. Some people think that the shape of the pyramids was inspired by the high place where the first god appeared and began the work of creation. Pyramids were built for the glory of the early pharaohs, and to protect their dead bodies. Inside them, granite doors and dead-end passages were built to stop thieves from stealing the riches buried with the pharaoh. Later pharaohs were buried in tombs dug into the rocky sides of the **Valley of the Kings**. The usual plan of these tombs consisted of a long corridor dug into the earth and ending in a burial chamber. Royal wives and children were buried nearby in the **Valley of the Queens**.

• The ancient Egyptians worshipped many gods, who were often shown with animals' heads. The sun god was very important, and had several names. At dawn he was the beetle-headed **Khepri**; at other times he was called **Ra** or **Atum**. Sometimes he was associated with the creator god **Amun** and became **Amun-Ra**. **Osiris** was the god of the dead, and ruled the Underworld with his wife **Isis**. His son **Horus**, who had a falcon's head, was the god of kingship. **Anubis**, the jackal god, protected the cemeteries, while **Thoth**, represented by the ibis bird, was the patron of scribes. **Bastet**, the cat-goddess, was the daughter of Ra.